began to joke and giggle until there were . . .

9 **Nine naughty fairies dancing until late,**

one fell asleep and then there were . . .

8 **Eight excited fairies bought cakes from 'Cake Heaven',**

one ate one too many so then there were . . .

7 Seven sparkly fairies practising their flicks,

one flicked her wand away and then there were . . .

6 Six sneaky fairies peeping in a hive,

one was too nosey so then there were . . .

5 **Five fancy fairies with make-up galore,**

one wore mum's lipstick and then there were . . .

 **Four fun-filled fairies playing by the sea,**

one got wet and sandy so then there were . . .

3 Three crafty fairies making things with glue,

one got far too sticky and then there were . . .

2 Two tired fairies sitting in the sun,

one went in for tea so then there was

1

One wistful fairy who soon began to wriggle,

so back flew all her friends for yet another . . . .

Other Ragged Bears books that you might enjoy!

10

8

7

9

Ten Terrible Dinosaurs

Paul Stickland

ISBN 1 85714 212 8
£4.99 • PB

ISBN 1 85714 353 1
£3.99

ISBN 1 85714 310 8
£3.99

ISBN 1 85714 334 5
£3.99 • PB

ISBN 1 85714 332 9
£3.99 • PB

ISBN 1 85714 276 4
£4.99 • PB

ISBN 978 1 85714 373 7
£4.99 • PB

Available from our website www.raggedbears.co.uk or telephone 01963 34300 to be sent a full catalogue.